Larry L. King's

NO REWARD!

PublishAmerica
Baltimore

ISBN: 1-4137-4512-1
PUBLISHED BY PUBLISHAMERICA, LLLP
www.publishamerica.com
Baltimore

Printed in the United States of America

DEDICATION

During a Monday night visitation program from my church, a fellow deacon and I rang the doorbell at Wanda Eckman's home. This was in July 1997 and she had been recently widowed, as was I. She made quite an impression on me and I was unable to get her out of my mind, not that I wanted to. After several attempts to call her and losing my nerve, I finally left a message on her answering machine. When she returned my call, after several minutes of beating around the bush, I asked her if she would have dinner with me. I was just a little rusty asking for a date, but she said yes and we started dating in August. I knew from the start that she was special and I wanted our relationship to go on forever.

We were married January 10, 1998, and I must say she has been a great motivator for me. I started making up and telling her bedtime stories while we were lying in bed at night. The subject matter varied from night to night, but was never X-rated. She said she enjoyed the stories. I hope she did because it encouraged me to put some of these thoughts on paper. I asked her to perform the task of proofreading my stories. That is not an easy task because my thoughts often outrun my slow-typing fingers. Words would be left out and very confusing at times. Wanda is always the prototype for the women in my stories. The men in my stories are head over heels in love with their ladies, as I am with Wanda. Without her help and support, none of my stories would be complete or completed. Thanks, Wanda. I love you more than the words of a mere mortal man can express.

—Larry

TABLE OF CONTENTS

World War II 7

War's Over—Back to School 15

The Plan 21

Plan in Motion 31

Torrey Pines 35

Back to the Drawing Board 39

Year Two 43

What's Next 53

Mike's First Race 59

Romance at Last 63

Christmas 71

1952 LeMans 75

Senior Year 85

Dreams Shattered 91

Rebuilding 97

Revisited 103

WORLD WAR II

In 1935, Simon Spangler opened a small auto repair shop in Santee, California, on the outskirts of San Diego. He built and repaired performance cars for wealthy young men in the area and kept up repairs on their family's sedans. He operated his business in the same manner as he lived his life: with a high code of integrity and honesty. Although he possessed sterling qualities, his heart was weak because of rheumatic fever as a child. He enjoyed racing his own car, a modified midget chassis with a Ford V8-60 engine and a modified Crosley body. I worked for Simon Spangler. I learned auto mechanics from him at an early age. He was my dad. My mother passed away when I was only three and from the time I was big enough to hold a wrench, I worked with my dad. However, he never let me work on cars until my schoolwork was done. Almost every weekend we went from dirt track to dirt track racing that

Ford. When I got older he allowed me to race in some events.

During the latter part of 1938, Artie Shaw had a big hit song, "Begin the Beguine." My dad loved that song and every morning he would put it on the phonograph at seven in the morning. That was the sound that woke me every day for months.

On the first day of December 1938, when I woke up, I sensed something was different. It was after nine o'clock in the morning and there was no Artie Shaw record playing on the phonograph. It was a bright sunny day and it was not like my dad to sleep late. I went in to wake him and discovered that he had died peacefully during the night. He was only forty-five, but his heart finally gave out. I was twenty-one and my best friend, my dad, had passed away.

During those days of working and racing, we were rarely apart. Life was not going to be the same without my dad around. I would miss his wit, wisdom, and his encouragement. I tried to keep the shop open for a while, but my heart wasn't in it. I sold the shop and the land it was located on to the Ford dealership located next to the shop.

In a few weeks I decided I wanted to see more of the world, so in early 1939, I joined the Marine Corps. I asked my friend, Bob, if I could keep the Ford in his garage until I returned from the service.

After my basic training, I was assigned to the Second Marine Air Wing under Brigadier General Ross E. Rowell at San Diego as an aircraft mechanic. I had joined the Marines to see the world and now I was back in my hometown. However, that would not last long.

In January of 1941, I was assigned to Marine Air Group 21 at Ewa, Hawaii. By now I was a master sergeant training young Marines on aircraft maintenance. The next four years changed the course of my life and our nation as well. Sunday, December 7, 1941, at 0755, two squadrons of Japanese fighters swept in from the northwest on low-altitude strafing runs blasting the parked planes with both cannons and machine guns. The strafing runs were repeated again and again until all aircraft were destroyed. Four Marines from MAG-21 were killed in the attack, and thirteen more were wounded. Of the forty-eight planes, thirty-three were demolished, with the remainder, except one, suffering major damage. One R3D transport was at Ford Island for repairs and somehow escaped damage in the attacks there.

The attack at Ewa was simultaneous with similar attacks on Pearl Harbor and Hickam Field on the island of Oahu. At Ewa, every Marine plane was knocked out of action in the first attack. The airplanes were not widely dispersed because a general warning about the possibility of sabotage had been issued just hours before, and planes were parked near the runways, away from the perimeters of the field area to protect them from any local action on the ground. This made the aircraft easy targets from an air attack.

Fortunately, no carriers were in port on December 7. The USS Enterprise was on the way back from Wake Island where she had delivered twelve F4F Wildcat fighters of VMF-211, and USS Lexington was en route to Midway with eighteen SB2U-3 Vindicator scout bombers of

VMSB-231. One thing was unquestionably clear; the nation was in for a long and bitter war.

VMF-214 was commissioned early in 1942 at Ewa. In August of 1943, twenty-seven young men under Gregory "Pappy" Boyington's leadership formed the original "Black Sheep" of VMF-214. Before U.S. involvement in the war, Major Boyington had volunteered for the "Flying Tigers" American Volunteer Group in China where the pilots were promised $675 a month plus $500 for every enemy plane they downed. Major Boyington was only thirty years old when the Black Sheep were formed; this was a little old for a combat pilot, thus he received the nickname "Pappy."

In the early part of World War II, flyers occasionally cropped that were unattached and separated from their squadrons for various reasons. Because of illness or breakup of their organizations, these flyers had been lost in the shuffle and had no way of getting back into the fight. Some were veteran combat pilots with several kills to their credit; others were pilots newly arrived from the United States as replacements. All were eager to join a squadron and see action against the Japanese; their efforts were met with refusals and orders to sit and wait. This was the situation at Espiritu Santo, New Hebrides, when finally the persistent campaigning of Major Boyington and Major Stan Bailey (Major Bailey was later named executive officer) was rewarded when wing headquarters gave them permission to form the stragglers into a squadron, with the understanding that they would have less than four weeks to mold themselves into a fully trained, completely coordinated Marine squadron. This was accomplished by flying every day and night with their eight Corsairs. It was my job to keep Pappy's Black Sheep aircraft in flying condition.

They flew their first combat mission on September 16, 1943, escorting Dauntless dive-bombers to Ballale, a small island west of Bougainville where the Japanese had a heavily fortified airstrip. They encountered heavy opposition from the enemy Zeros, and Pappy claimed five kills, his best single-day total. The Black Sheep fought their way to fame in just eighty-four days, piling up a record of 197 aircraft destroyed or damaged, troop transports and supply ships sunk, and ground installations destroyed in addition to numerous other victories.

In October the VMF-214 group moved from their original base in the Russells to a more advanced location at Munda. From here they were closer to the next big objective, the Japanese bases on Bougainville. On one mission over Bougainville, according to Major Boyington, the Japanese radioed him in English, asking him to report his position and so forth. Pappy played along, but stayed 5000 feet higher than he had told them, and when the Zeros came along, the Black Sheep blew twelve of them away. The absolute veracity of Boyington's account is not certain, but that's how he told the story. One night with a quarter moon, he went up to try to deal with "Washing Machine Charlie," but without results.

Anyone who has spent the night at our base on Munda is familiar with Washing Machine Charlie, the Japanese scout plane with a noisy engine. "Charlie" wasn't much of a threat with only two small bombs strapped to the wings.

He flew in low and attempted to release his bombs on our runway. Often in the darkness, he confused the beach for the runway and dropped his load harmlessly on an empty beach. If someone got lucky and shot him down, he wasn't missed as the Japanese had plenty of Charlies. The next night another Charlie took his place.

The Pacific War was the largest naval conflict in history. Across the huge expanses of the Pacific, the two most powerful navies in the world found themselves locked in a death struggle. The war was fought in every possible climate, from Arctic conditions in the Aleutians, to the appalling heat and swelter of the South Pacific. Every conceivable type of naval activity was represented: carrier aviation battles, surface engagements, bitterly fought night-fights, the largest amphibious landings of the entire war, and the stealthy, brutal battles waged by and against submarines.

With the likelihood of the war's end approaching and the invasion of Japan by allied forces seeming to be a reality, concern was given to the tenacity of the Japanese forces to fight to the death. The battles for the other islands in the Pacific had been won with many Allied casualties.

President Roosevelt died on April 12, 1945, only a few weeks after being sworn in as the President of the United States for an unprecedented fourth term. The President was stricken with a cerebral hemorrhage and died while sitting for a portrait in Warm Springs, Georgia. During his twelve years as president, he had not only battled the ravages of his physical afflictions, but also endured the

Great Depression and World War II. Harry S. Truman scarcely saw President Roosevelt during his few weeks as vice president and received no briefing on the development of the atomic bomb or the unfolding difficulties with Soviet Russia. Suddenly these and a host of other wartime problems became Truman's to solve when, on April 12, 1945, he became president. He told reporters, "I felt like the moon, the stars, and all the planets had fallen on me." As President, Truman made some of the most crucial decisions in history. Soon after the victory in Europe, the war against Japan had reached its final stage. An urgent plea to Japan to surrender was rejected. Truman, after consultations with his advisers, ordered atomic bombs dropped on cities devoted to war work.

The unit selected for this dangerous mission was the 509th Composite Group commanded by Colonel Paul W. Tibbets, Jr. Colonel Tibbets flew the first atomic bomb mission to Hiroshima on August 6, 1945. Records show that his aircraft was named in honor of his mother, "Enola Gay" Tibbets. The bombing mission was a success, and a second bomb was dropped on Nagasaki three days later. Within a week, Japan was ready to surrender.

The Japanese signed the official Instrument of Surrender on September 2, 1945, aboard the USS *Missouri* as it was anchored in Tokyo Bay.

The war was over and we were going home. Most of my group arrived back in San Diego in February of 1946. It was both a happy and sad occasion for me. As I watched the reunion of families and the men I had fought with, I felt alone because there was no one to greet me. My father was the only family I had ever known and many of these young men had become like my family, but now they had been reunited with their real families. It was good to see their joy!

WAR'S OVER—
BACK TO SCHOOL

During the war I realized how much I enjoyed teaching those young men and decided to return to school. My ambition was to become a teacher. I was twenty-nine years old and starting a career late in life as many war veterans did.

I enrolled at the University of San Diego in September of 1946 to pursue a degree in education and automotive engineering. I moved back to Santee, where my father's shop had been located. That meant a 20-mile commute each day to the university. As classes began and I was becoming familiar with the campus, I had a pleasant surprise. Hap Johnson was one of my classmates. We had shared living quarters in the South Pacific during the war and our bond became even stronger during our school days together. His father was a professor at the university. Hap and his father provided a family atmosphere that had been missing since my dad's passing. Hap's father gave me the same type of help that my dad had given. Hap's father could cheer me up when I was down and give me encouragement when I wanted to give up.

With the help of my GI bill to pay for school and the guidance of Hap's father, I was able to graduate in three and a half years. The next phase of my life was about to begin and it would be the most challenging and happiest in many years.

In the fall of 1950, I started my teaching career at Mission Bay High School in San Diego. My schedule included four mathematic classes and an auto mechanics class. As a first-year teacher many adjustments had to be made and much was to be learned from my fellow teachers. Some of my students were not eager to learn and needed serious motivation. Teaching a class they enjoyed, auto mechanics, should be an easy task. However, becoming involved with the rebel of the class was a challenge.

John Michael Brock II was seventeen years old and thought there was nothing more for him to learn; he already knew it all. He had no desire to attend school and thought my classes would be easy because I was a new teacher. He came from a wealthy family from the Bay Park area of San Diego. In an attempt to reach him, I arranged a meeting with his parents.

I arrived at the Brocks' home on Hartford Street at seven o'clock Wednesday evening. A stone and iron fence surrounded the large two-story house. The grounds were landscaped and well manicured. It was about a quarter mile drive from the street to the house. I turn off the engine and sat in the truck for a moment gazing at this beautiful home. It looked like a movie set. I walked to the door and rang the doorbell. A woman in her mid fifties greeted me at the door. She was wearing a gray dress and a white apron. She introduced herself as Mildred, the maid, then escorted me to the parlor to announce my arrival. This beautifully tanned lady wearing a simple white dress entered the room. I had never seen such beauty, except in the movies. Many thoughts ran through my head before she spoke. My first thought was how attractive she was. My second was this must be Mike's sister. That thought was incorrect.

"Mr. Spangler, I'm Rosemary Brock, Mike's mother."

I was surprised that she was Mike's mother and maybe some of my thoughts were inappropriate. "Mrs. Brock, it is a pleasure to meet you," I responded. I almost said, "I thought you were Mike's sister," but thought better of it and did not include the second remark.

"Please call me Rose."

"Yes, Rose, and please call me Simon. You have a very lovely home. I enjoyed the drive from the street to the house; the colors of the flowers and the grounds are beautiful. I wanted to talk to both you and Mike's father. Will Mr. Brock be joining us this evening?"

"No, Mike's father is gone."

"I'm sorry, maybe we should reschedule when he returns."

"Mr. Spangler, I'm sorry, Simon. When I said he was gone, I meant he has passed away."

"I'm sorry to hear that. Was it during the war?"

"Yes, he was killed in the South Pacific. He was a Marine pilot and was shot down during the Battle of Midway. Only one pilot from his group survived the battle. That was eight years ago."

"The war caused boys to become men far too soon and many to die much too young. The Battle of Midway was a terrible battle and was the turning point in the war, thanks to men like your husband. I served with the 214th Marine Air Group as an aircraft mechanic. The pilots that I knew were very brave and I'm sure your husband was also. It is unfortunate that so many had to die and we'll always be in their debt. Sometimes I have survivor's guilt. Others lost their lives and left families to cope with the loss. I have no family and would not have been missed. How did Mike react to his father's death?"

"I don't think you should say no one would miss you. I'm sure you have many friends that would have missed you very much. Mike was eight when Richard, that was his father, went away. They had been very close and at first, Mike was very proud his father was a Marine flyer. As the war drug on Mike's troubles seemed to increase. He became more and more bitter about his father being gone. Richard's father operated a manufacturing plant and wanted Richard to stay and help with the plant operation, but Richard felt he needed to be more actively involved in the war. They manufactured gas masks and other war materials after the war started. Richard was more of a hands-on man. Richard's father was very bitter with Richard's decision and I'm afraid some of that rubbed off on Mike after awhile."

"Yes." I responded, "this is the time in a young man's life when a father is very important. At that age my father and I were racing his old Ford on the weekends and having the time of our lives. My father died when I was twenty-one and I still miss him and those days we spent together. I want to help Mike. At one time I was a lot like Mike and my dad helped me a great deal. What do you suggest that I do to reach him? Do you have any ideas how to do that?"

"So far Mike's problems have not gotten him into serious trouble, but I fear if he does not get his life straight, he is headed for bigger problems. His grandfather and I have tried all that we know to do and have gotten nowhere!"

"Please excuse me for asking, but is there a male role model for Mike? Perhaps his grandfather or a friend of yours?" I hope that did not sound to her like it sounded to me. A friend of hers? That sounded like I wanted to ask her out on a date. *Simon, think about what you are saying!*

"No, there isn't anyone. His grandfather is somewhat disabled and can't help much and I have no men in my life."

"I certainly don't wish to presume that I am a good role model, but my dad and I were very happy when we were racing. What do you think of a class project of working on my old racecar? That might change Mike's outlook."

"I'm not to sure about that, but it does deserve some consideration," Rose responded without a lot of enthusiasm.

Maybe it wasn't a great idea, but it worked for me and my dad and and it might work for Mike too. "Let me do some planning and get back with you."

"Yes, do that, Simon, and thanks for taking an interest in Mike. I look forward to our next meeting."

"Rose, it was a pleasure to meet you. Mike is very fortunate to have a mother like you."

As I was driving away from their house, my thoughts returned to those fond days spent with my father years ago. Things seemed much different then as we worked hard and played harder. Would I ever feel that much life again?

THE PLAN

There were many problems to overcome and decisions to be made. Prior to World War II, the Automobile Racing Club of America (ARCA) had handled road racing in the United States. ARCA suspended activities at the beginning of U.S. involvement in World War II in 1941. Everyone assumed they would resume after the war, but so far that had not happened. Dad and I participated in dirt track events with the Ford and were very competitive. Drag racing's roots were planted on dry lakebeds like Muroc in California's Mojave Desert, where hot rodders had congregated since the early 1930s and speeds first topped 100-mph drag racing in California. The Ford would be suited to that type of racing. If a school project were to take place, funds would be limited and the Ford was all I had to work with.

Many of the men stationed in England during the war had developed a love for the British sports cars. Some bought MGs and Jaguars during their stay in England. After the war when they returned to the States, they brought their cars with them. Hill climbing events were popular in England. Hill climbing events were run up a rugged uphill course in a race against the clock. The quickest time won! Some of the American service men had become involved in these events and sought some type of competition after returning home. Road racing had its infancy on abandoned airstrips. The Ford would have done well in hill climbing events, but none existed in the States. It would also be suited for drag racing. However, the road racing had a stronger appeal to me.

The first thing I needed to do was to bring my car home from my friend's garage. I called Bob and asked how much dust had built up on the car. I had not seen or talked to him since we shipped out for the war. Bob had become a pilot and assigned to the 8th Army Air Corps stationed in England and was one of those who returned with the love of the British sports cars. He had an MG TC. It was a wonderful machine with 17" wire wheels and a spunky four-cylinder engine. We caught up on what was happening in our lives and of our plans for the future. Bob had recently married and had started a job as a test pilot. I made arrangements to pick up the car. I told Bob about my plans for a project for my students and my objective of reaching Mike and other rebels in the class. Bob liked my plan and thought it might work. He offered to help in any way he could.

I towed the car home and cleaned out a place for it in the garage. The next step was to clean the fuel tank and change the oil in the engine. The cleaning process took a week and now it was time to start the engine after many years of storage. The sound of the open exhaust was music to my ears. This sound filled me with excitement and thoughts of my dad. I could almost hear him say, "The carb needs to be a little richer!" I made the adjustment and said to myself, "Thanks, Dad." I ventured out onto the street for a quick lap around the block before neighbors called the police to complain about the noise. It was fun to drive it again, but it needed a lot of work to be in race shape again.

After about two weeks of thinking, I had a preliminary plan worked out in my mind. Saturday, I called Mrs. Brock to outline my plan to her. "Rose, this is Simon. I would like to see you and discuss my project."

"I thought you might have forgotten about it since I hadn't heard from you! Why don't you come for dinner tonight and we can discuss what you have in mind. Mike is gone for the weekend and we can keep our meeting secret until you are ready to present it to your students."

"Thanks for the invitation. I was beginning to get tired of hot dogs and sandwiches. I really must learn to cook! Would about seven o'clock be fine?"

"Yes, that would be fine, see you then."

I must admit dinner with Rose sounded very good. As interested as I was about getting Mike set on a straight course—well, Mike was the main issue, but Rose had my attention also.

I arrived at the Brock Estate in my best suit and tie. Well, actually my only suit and tie. I felt like a complete fool; why did I dress like this? Before I got out of my old truck, I removed my coat and tie. I walked to the door and rang the bell.

Mildred answered the door. "Good evening, Mr. Spangler. The family is waiting for you in the parlor."

The family? What was that about? Mike was not supposed to be here. Rose was standing by the sofa and an older gentleman was in a big leather chair to her right. As I entered the room I noticed crutches by his chair. He spoke first. "You must be Mr. Spangler. I am Michael's grandfather, John Brock. Please excuse me for not standing. I had a bout with polio several years ago and it left me a little immobile. Rose has told me you have taken an interest in Michael. I asked if it would be all right for me to be here tonight and hear your plans. Please sit here next to me."

There was another leather chair closer to the sofa where Rose would take a seat. I sat down, trying not to show my surprise to see him here and for the moment speechless. I quickly gathered my thoughts but started to babble. "Mr. Brock...this is an unexpected...uh...it is a pleasure to meet you, sir." I thought, *That was real smooth, Simon, you're going have to do better than that to sell your plans to this man.* Quickly I said, "Mr. Brock, during my days in combat in the Pacific, I saw Brock Enterprises on many of our supply shipments. Are you that John Brock?"

"Yes, my companies made many war supplies, from bullets to bandages and gas masks to bed linens. Our main products today are containers of this new substance called plastic."

"It is a pleasure and honor to meet you. I think without men like you back home, we would never have won the war! The country is fortunate to have men with your industrial strengths."

Rose interrupted and asked, "Simon, would you like a drink before dinner?"

"No thanks, Rose, I don't drink." I thought, *Why did you add the last remark? Did it sound as if I disapproved of the drink they were having?* After seeing how they were dressed for dinner, suddenly I felt underdressed. Mr. Brock was dressed in a blue suit and Rose was dressed in a beige dress. Mr. Brock still had an athletic appearance despite his condition. Rose looked very stunning in her dress and a string of pearls around her neck. I should have left my coat and tie on.

Mildred entered the room and announced dinner. I almost made another mistake; Mr. Brock was struggling to get to his feet and I started to help him up. I saw a look on Rose's face as if to say, "He wants to do it by himself."

As he steadied himself he said, "I hope you like roasted lamb with mint jelly."

"Yes, that's one of my favorites." I had never had lamb in my life and all of the sudden it's my favorite! I was a beef and potato man.

Mr. Brock took the seat at the head of the table, Rose was on his left, while I sat to his right opposite Rose. As we enjoyed the meal, I found myself staring at Rose. I hoped no one noticed, but she was so beautiful I could not take my eyes off her. She was very captivating. The lamb was delicious and after a wonderful dessert, I have no idea what it was, Mr. Brock again struggled to his feet and suggested we have coffee in the parlor. "Mr. Spangler, I am eager to hear your plan."

Once in the parlor we resumed the same seating as before dinner. As Mr. Brock took his seat, he allowed a heavy sigh to come out as if he were very tired. "Mr. Spangler," he said, "in my youth I ran track; however, I'm afraid my days of the forty-yard dash are over. Please tell me of your plan." All of this seemed to be as important to him as if we were discussing a corporate merger or a new product line. He was so very business like that I was disappointed my presentation didn't include charts and graphs.

"Mr. Brock, please call me Simon."

"And please call me John."

"Yes, sir, John it is." I was beginning to feel much more comfortable. "John, Rose, I'm afraid this is not much of a plan, it's more of a concept. I can only relate to my own experience and the turning point in my life. I lost my mother when I was very young. Growing up with my father oftentimes was difficult. We had very little in the way of luxuries. I had a time of rebellion just as Mike is having now. Growing up in the shadow of my father's auto repair shop, my interest of course was cars. My dad had this car, an old modified midget we called 'The Ford' that he raced on dirt tracks in the area. During my high school days, my grades began to fall. For that reason my dad stopped taking me with him to the races. I wanted to be with him, but I had to stay home and study. My father and I made a deal. If I brought my grades up, then I could go racing with him again. If my grades suffered, I stayed home. I became a teacher because I enjoy shaping young men's lives. I teach mathematics and an auto mechanics class at Mission Bay. Several students in my class lost their dads in the war and are struggling with life with only a mother. My life without a mother was difficult and I'm sure life for boys without a father would be even more difficult. I don't desire to become a father to all these boys, but I do want them to become better students and hopefully I can be a role model for them. My father's plan was simple: good grades, go racing, bad grades, stay home. I still have the Ford and would like to involve some of my students in an after-school program. We would work on the car after school and find a track to race on the weekend. My father's plan would apply to each one: good grades, go racing, bad grades, stay home. It's pretty simple, I know, but it worked for me and maybe it will work for them."

John looked at Rose and Rose looked back at him. Then they both looked at me. Rose spoke first. "Simon, we have tried everything and nothing has worked. I am willing to try, but the boys don't drive, okay?"

"I could not agree more, I'll drive and they can handle the pit crew duties." I looked at John and he nodded his approval.

With our business concluded, John struggled to his feet. "It's been a long day. I think I'll retire for the night and leave the evening to you young people. Goodnight, Rose. Simon, I look forward to seeing you again."

John excused himself and went upstairs.

"Simon, John likes you," Rose told me after he had left.

"How can you tell?"

"He has a certain look when he approves and over the years I have come to recognize it. I remember the first time I noticed that look in his approval of me."

"I was surprised to see John here tonight. I had no idea that he lived here."

"When Richard and I got married, we had a small house on the north side of town. When he left for the service, we sold the house and I moved here. This estate has been in the family for years. John's father built this house back in the eighteen hundreds. I'm sorry if you were uncomfortable tonight."

"I was at first, I guess you could tell that by my stammering. I like John too. He seems straightforward and honest. I'll bet he's a good man to work for."

"He has been very successful and it is not because he is a ruthless businessman, but rather because he is hard working and cares about his people. His employees have responded to his type of management and work very hard for him."

It was obvious how much Rose loved and cared for this man.

"Rose, I have had a wonderful time tonight, but I need to head back to Santee and prepare for my presentation to the class on Monday. I want to make it sound exciting without over selling the idea."

Rose walked me to the door. "Simon, I had a good time also, the best I've had in a long time. Thanks for coming."

"Goodnight, Rose." I turned and started to walk toward my truck.

"Simon," she said and I turned to look at her, "I couldn't take my eyes off you either."

Well, so much for no one noticing, but I didn't mind now.

PLAN IN MOTION

Monday came quickly and I was excited about the prospect of racing again and getting these young men involved. My goal was to make a difference in the way they viewed life and show them how exciting life could be. More than anything, I wanted them to believe that with hard work there was nothing they could not do.

I had a hard time waiting for my auto mechanics class that afternoon; it seemed to be a much longer day than normal. I had twelve boys in the class and we were approaching the end of the first six weeks of school. They were a combination of sophomores and juniors. Mike was a sophomore and none of these boys were the least bit interested in school.

"Guys, I know you took this class because you like cars and you thought it would be an easy class. I'm glad you like cars, but this class will not be easy. I am going to require

31

you to learn about why and how a car works. Analyze problems and how to solve them. How many of you would be interested in going to the races and I don't mean as spectators, but as participants?" All their eyes lit up for the first time this school year.

"Here's the deal! I have an old car that my dad and I raced back in the late thirties. It's old and not very fast by today's standards. I need some help fixin' it up and help in the pit crew. Here's the catch, guys. Your grades are not very good and I need smart guys on my crew. We can start work on the car and you will have another six weeks to bring your grades up, then we go racing. If you have homework to do, that must be done before you work on the car."

Mike was the first to speak. "Mr. Spangler, count me in." Five more also wanted to be involved. It just happened to be those boys who did not have a dad at home. I hoped this gamble worked.

For the first few weeks we worked in my garage. The twenty-mile commute from school to my house in Santee made it difficult for the boys to work except on weekends. Mike approached me with an idea, and as it turned out it was a very good idea.

"Mr. Spangler, we have an old carriage house at our place that would make an excellent shop and it's close to all the guys. They can walk to my house and we can work on the car after school and the weekends. I've already checked with my mother and grandfather; they both agreed it would be a good place to work."

I agreed and we made plans to move the car to the carriage house. Much of the car had been disassembled and parts were everywhere. Mike asked his grandfather to help move the car. John sent a large truck and some of his shipping guys to move the car and all the pieces. After it had all been loaded, I asked the men to put the tools in the truck. Mike said that would not be necessary. I was in for a big surprise when we arrived at the Brock Estate. The carriage house was large enough for six cars. John had already converted it to a shop. My dad would love to have had a shop like this back in the old days. The place was spotless with a black-and-white tile floor that looked like a checkered flag. Every tool that we would possibly need was there. Drill press, gear pullers, lathes, and even a milling machine were here. There was a tool chest for each guy and most important, over in the corner of the shop was a study area for them to do their homework before working on the car. John had spent a small fortune to outfit this shop and I could never thank him enough for what he was doing. At the end of the next six-week semester everyone's grades had improved at least one grade and some two. The car was back together again. They had done their part; now I started to look for a place to go racing. My friend, Bob, stopped by the shop to view our progress. He was driving his MG. This was the first British sports car the boys had ever seen. They examined every inch of it and asked Bob a thousand questions. He told me about some races at Torrey Pines where he planned to race his car.

TORREY PINES

The first race held at Torrey Pines was in 1949 and it was only about twenty miles from San Diego. This was the second year of the event and it was exciting to be around racing again. I don't know who was more thrilled to be there, the guys or me. I tried not to show a lot of apprehension, but this was my first time with this sort of racing and my first race of any kind in many years. It would be much different than dirt track racing. First of all, it was run on pavement. Second, it had many turns left and right instead of only left-hand turns on an oval track.

The first turn at Torrey Pines was a 90-degree turn to the left on to a straight in the direction of the ocean, then two turns to the right heading back east. After a short straight, a fast turn back left and right again, another right turn followed the short straight on to the back straight. It had a kink or two in it and that is putting it mildly! It is taken flat out in all but the fastest cars before having to brake hard for the two right turns and head back to the start-finish line where the spectator area was located.

It was obvious that our car was not fast that day. Cars with much smaller engines, including Bob's MG, and less top speed were passing me because they took the corners much better. The fastest cars on the straight don't always win the race. The car to beat that day was Tom Carsten's Allard J2. During the next two years this car would become a legend as it won eight major races in a row. Wins included races at Golden Gate Park, Torrey Pines, Reno, and Pebble Beach. Tom has a sense of style and it showed in the car's presentation. The glossy black automobile was finished with red interior, and all visible suspension parts were painted red. Mounted-on custom-made red Borrianni wire wheels with wide whitewall tires. Our fifteen-year-old car was no match for the Allard or even the MG TCs. I continued to do my best, driving the car to its limits and mine as well. In the fourth hour of the six-hour event, the engine gave out and we failed to finish. We got our first DNF (did not finish).

After getting the car back to the pits, I could see the disappointment on the boys' faces. I was disappointed also, not so much for the outcome of the race but because the way the boys had prepared, they deserved better results. This experience had not gone well, but we had learned from our mistakes. I made no excuses and simply said, "Okay, now for the homework. I need a report Monday on what we did right, what we did wrong, and how we can improve. Thanks for your hard work, guys. Let's pack it up and go home."

We loaded the car onto the trailer and headed back to the shop. We all were disappointed, but I hoped that we all had profited from the day.

BACK TO THE DRAWING BOARD

By Monday afternoon the boys were ready to get back to work. Class time was spent on rebuilding carburetors and the past weekend was not mentioned. Each one had rebounded and acted as if nothing had gone wrong at Torrey Pines. After school and homework was done, we began to discuss the race.

Mike was the leader of the bunch and spoke for them. "As I see it we were not only slow, but unreliable. To win a race you have to finish the race. Our car was definitely not the best car on the track, but we can make it better."

"Mike, I could not agree with you more. However, this is the only car we have and yes, we can make it better."

We started with the engine, although it was not the major problem. The flathead engine was converted to overhead valve with Ardun conversions and a four-barrel carburetor. We had no dyno, but we probably were making over two hundred horsepower, doubling the original one hundred horsepower. We modified the chassis by lowering the car and widening the tread width. Stiffer springs and heaver shocks were added. Just to make it look better, we changed the body and painted it red. Not being a superstitious person, the car was trimmed with a black number thirteen on a white circle background. We were ready for the next event.

March Air Force Base was our next race 115 miles to the north, near Riverside, California. We still would not be the fastest car, but our desire for a good finish overshadowed any thoughts of an all-out win. Our work had not gone in vain. We were faster and more dependable. We raced in three events that weekend and finished all races. Our best finish was a sixth place in the main event, which was easily won by Tom Carsten's Allard J2. We had several more races that year at various tracks and our car at least proved to be consistent. Our last race for the year was at Pebble Beach. It was 140 miles from home and another long trip. We ended the year on a good finish. We got a first place in one of the preliminary events and finished the main event closing in on the fourth place car. A fifth place was our best finish in a main event race. Even though school was out and racing for the season was over, the boys continued to hang out at the shop working on the car, if only to wash and polish. They all began to read books on chassis design and hot-rodding. Their studies also expanded into all their schoolwork. They had turned the corner and wanted to learn all they could. My first year as a teacher had been a good one, a very good one.

YEAR TWO

Having such a good first year, I had high expectations for our second year. I had some new students in my math classes as well as the auto class. A few more boys became involved with the afternoon program, but not on a consistent basis. The original boys remained faithful to our racing team. We were a very close group, but remained open to new members for the program. The fire of racing was not there for any of my new students; they did, however, benefit from the mentoring and fellowship with the other boys.

We dusted off the car for another season with high hopes for a good year. I must admit I was pleased with the progress these young men had made in just one short year. If we did no better than last year, I would be happy. I had done what I wanted to do: light a fire under these guys and help them learn how exciting knowledge can be. Rose told me she was pleased with the change in Mike and the results of the past year. John expressed that he was equally pleased.

Our first outing in 1951 would be at Torrey Pines again. This was our second time to race here and the third annual race at The Pines. We hoped for better results this year. We had a full year of racing behind us and had done well for a bunch of kids with a limited budget. Things could only be better.

We entered all the races scheduled for the weekend and had much better results this year. I was not ready for what was to come next. Monday, we were all at the shop and the phone rang. Mike answered because he had the cleanest hands at the time. "Sarge, Daddy Brock wants you to come up to the house." They started calling me Sarge near the end of last year. I think they thought they were in the Marines themselves. It was always "Semper Fi, Sarge" for everything. Mike's grandfather had become Daddy Brock to all the boys.

"Okay, tell him I'll be there in a few minutes." As I was washing my hands, I wondered what he could want or wanted to say. All had gone well at Torrey Pines; the car was fine and running well.

John maintained an office in the library located in the back part of the house. As I walked in, I noticed some papers on his desk. His desk was normally clean of any clutter and only his current project would be the desk. Not that I tried, but I could not or didn't notice what the papers were.

He glanced through the papers as he spoke. "Simon, please have a seat, there is something I want to discuss with you."

Still in a state of confusion, I sat down. "What's up, John?"

He continued to look at the papers in his hand. "Nothing really, I just wanted to run something by you and get your thoughts."

"Sure, I would be happy to," I responded with what I am sure was a puzzled look.

"Simon, you and the lads did very well last year and they have matured more than I could have imagined. I am very satisfied with all you have done with Mike and the other boys."

"Thanks, but I notice a bit of something…I'm not sure where you are going with this conversation."

"Don't be alarmed. I'm trying to ask if you want to move to the next level."

"I'm sorry, sir, I don't know what the next level is. We have done what we set out to do and the rest is just having fun."

"Simon, don't get me wrong. I'm happy with last year. It's just that I have always been a competitor from running track to having a successful business. If I get involved in something, I want to get to the top. I'm only putting an idea before you. Rose and I were at all the races last year and this guy with the Allard seems to be the man to beat. I want to know if you want to compete at that level."

"John, I don't think I understand what you're getting at."

"Let me just say it plain and simple. You operated at your own expense last year and I'm sure that was not easy for you on a teacher's salary. I am prepared to form a company to finance your racing operation and purchase a new car. An Allard if that's the best choice. I have papers here and we can get one for less than $3,000 without an engine. You can get the best engine available and I will fund the company with $50,000 to start."

"John, that sounds exciting, but my job is teaching, not racing. Racing was only a tool to reach these young men. I'm not sure what more could be accomplished by expanding the program."

"You're probably right, but give it some thought and let me know."

I returned to the shop and every eye in the room was on me. Mike spoke up and asked, "What did Daddy Brock want?"

"He wants to buy us a new race car."

"Wow, that would be great!" they all responded, and I could see I was going to be over-ruled and the Ford was going into retirement.

I made a call back to the house. "John, it looks like I've been out voted. Go ahead and order the car."

"Well, actually I placed the order two weeks ago, it will be here in another two weeks."

"I know I shouldn't ask, but what were you going to do with the car if I had said no?"

"I had two options: change your mind or sell the car and make a little money on the deal. I'm just glad it worked out this way."

"Just to be clear, John, I appreciate all that you are doing, but I was blind sided on this one and it was not pleasant. In the future, please keep me informed before you go forward with any plans. We, you and I, must work as a team. If you are not happy with me, just let me know and I will step aside. Teaching is my calling and the racing is just a tool to reach these boys. It is clear to me they want to be more competitive, but if their grades suffer—it's back to the books only."

"I could not agree more, Simon. I'm sorry for the way I handled this situation. It won't happen again. It is your program to run as you see fit. You have done so much for Rose, Mike, me, and the other lads. You all are like family now."

After a few days I had time to regroup. I called a friend who worked for Chrysler and asked whom I needed to talk to about getting an engine. Gene Turner was one of those young men I had trained in the South Pacific and now he was working in the research and development department of Chrysler.

"Simon, you old son of a gun. How long has it been, at least seven years?"

"Yes, it has been a long time, too long. How are things going with you at Chrysler?"

"We have a lot of interesting projects going at this time. Cars are changing more and more every day. What are you doing now?"

"I went back to school, got my degree in education and mechanical engineering. I'm teaching at Mission Bay High School in San Diego now. That brings me back to the engine. I started racing my dad's Ford with my students last year. Do you remember seeing the name Brock Enterprises on some of our supply shipments? The head of Brock Enterprises is John Brock. He is the grandfather of one of my students and he wants us to prepare a new car for this year. He has purchased an Allard for us and we need an engine for it. I've been reading a lot about these Hemi-engines you guys have now."

"Yes, I think this engine has a great future in racing. The engine is new for our 1951 models with 331 cubic inches and 235-horsepower. We are working on a 392 cubic inch with dual four barrels producing close to 400 HP. In theory you can't get either one at this time. We were working with Allard to provide this engine for their J2, but those talks failed to produce results. A few engines will be released soon. Give me your address and don't be surprised if one shows up at your place next week. If anyone asks, you don't know where it came from."

"Thanks, Gene. Come to California when you can and see what we do with it. I owe you one."

"Simon, the war hasn't been that long ago and I haven't forgotten that you saved my life at Munda. I still owe you plenty."

The next week we received the shipment. It not only contained a complete engine and three-speed heavy-duty transmission, it also came with four manuals and many extra parts. Without taking a complete inventory of the parts, I would say there was enough to build another engine and have parts leftover. A few hours later, Gene showed up. He just happened to be in California on vacation with two engineers from Chrysler. They briefed the boys on the engine and the boys immediately went to work on it.

"Gene, there was no invoice with the shipment. Will that come later?" I asked.

"Simon, how can I invoice you for something I didn't send?"

"Are you going to get into hot water over this, more importantly are me and the boys going to get in trouble?"

Gene laughed. "No, no one is going to get in trouble, just consider yourselves part of Chrysler's R&D Department.

Shortly after that visit, the Allard was delivered from the local Cadillac dealer. I didn't tell them it was destined for a Chrysler engine. We had a lot of work to do if the car was to be ready for the race at March AFB.

We worked late almost every night and I had dinner with Mike's family most of those nights. It was especially nice seeing Rose on a regular basis. By Wednesday night we had the engine installed. The engine mounts were placed as far back in the chassis as possible in order to get more weight to the rear of the car.

Thursday night the guys arrived and I asked, "Don't you guys have a test tomorrow?"

"You know we do, it's your math test."

"Better hit the books before we get started tonight."

"Aren't you going to give us some help for the test?"

"Sure, study hard!" I knew they were only kidding as each was well prepared for the test. On Thursday, finishing touches would be taken care of just one week before the race.

The next Thursday we loaded the car and equipment on the trailers and hitched the trailers to the trucks. We had everything ready to leave after school on Friday. We arrived at the base about nine Friday night. We stored the car in a hanger set aside for contestants and checked into a motel nearby.

When I woke up Saturday morning, the excitement was already building. It was a beautiful day, even by California standards. The sun was bright and the weather was mild, perfect conditions for a weekend of racing. About thirty minutes later, the boys were knocking on my door. They were just as eager to get started as I was. We grabbed a bite to eat at the coffee shop before going to the track. We unloaded the car and made some last-minute adjustments. Mike started the engine to let it warm up. Mike was getting out as I was putting on my helmet. As I was strapping my safety belt on, Mike asked, "How does the car sound?"

With the noise of the engine, I had to do a little lip reading and I replied, "Sounds good" as I gave him the thumbs up. After a few practice laps, I felt confident we could compete with anyone with our new car. We won the preliminary qualifying race with ease. After the qualifying event, Gene and the same engineers from Chrysler showed up in the pits. These guys were still on "vacation."

For the main event on Sunday, Tom Carsten and I were in the front row in our Allards. As we entered the first turn I was slightly ahead and leading the pack. By the end of the first lap, Tom had taken the lead. Rose was in the pits keeping our lap charts. As I went by the pits she held up a sign with –3, meaning Tom was three seconds ahead of me. On the next lap –4. I needed to pick up my speed. I thought that was all the car had, but I started braking just a little later for the turns and on the next lap I was only down 2 seconds. By lap 7, I was right on the back of Tom's Allard. I was in his slipstream and not more than six inches separated our cars. This is at speeds approaching 110 miles per hour on the long straight. Finally, I was able to pass him when he missed a shift coming out of turn five. Over the next thirty laps we swapped positions time and time again. Rose signaled me with one lap to go "-1, push." I had Tom's Allard directly in front of me and push is what I did. I'm sure that Tom thought I was pushing him; not more than a foot separated our cars and much of the last lap we were side by side.

Coming out of the last turn, headed for the finish line, Tom was ahead by half a car length. I thought our Chrysler engine had more power and I could pass his Cadillac-powered car; instead we crossed the finish line side by side and I didn't know if we had won or not. As I pulled back into the pits, Rose and the boys were jumping and shouting, making me think we had won. We had finished inches behind Tom, but still a great finish for a high school racing team. I was just as happy as everyone else in our pits. Gene congratulated us on our finish and said he and the engineers would be returning to Detroit. I already had some changes in my head for the car and the engine for the next race.

WHAT'S NEXT

We had little preparations to make for the next race at Pebble Beach. However, things don't always go as expected. I had banged up the bodywork a little with a few dings from encounters with hay bales in the turns, but those were quickly repaired and painted. We always wanted a fresh-looking car and kept the exterior as new looking as possible. We changed the gears for Pebble Beach to get a little more speed on the top end.

About a week before the race, the unexpected happened. I was replacing the tires with wider ones and dropped a wheel on my foot. There was no tire on the wheel and the steel edge of the wheel hit me squarely on the top of my foot. It put me to the floor in pain. Perry took a look at it and said, "Sarge, I think it's broken. We gotta get you to the emergency room." Perry was right, it was broken. Perry got his nickname of "Doc" with that incident. There was no way I could race at Pebble Beach and I told the boys we had to cancel.

At school the next day, Mike asked, "Do we really have to cancel the race?"

"Mike, there is no way that I can drive with my foot in a cast. I had a friend bring me to school today."

"Sarge, I can drive."

"Mike, you have never driven in competition before and I promised your mother when we started, the boys don't drive, and I won't break that promise. Our season is over."

"Is it alright with you if I ask her?"

"You can ask her, but I think you'll get the same answer."

"Okay, I'll take you home tonight, but we'll stop by the house first and ask her. Thanks, Sarge."

"Don't thank me, I said no. If you drive it will be because she says it's okay."

After school we headed for Mike's house to talk to Rose. He was excited and I knew he was going to be disappointed with his mother's answer.

Mike ran to the front door, not waiting for me to hobble along. "Mom!" he shouted as he ran through the front door.

"In here, Mike." After he came in the room, she could see the excitement on his face. "Slow down. What has gotten you so worked up?"

I was slow getting in the house, but I could hear their conversation. Rose saw me at the door and motioned me to come in. "Simon, how is your foot doing?"

"As long as I don't put weight on it, it's feels okay."

Mike couldn't wait any longer and interrupted. "Mom, I have something I want to ask you."

"Sure, Mike, go ahead."

"Mr. Spangler said we have to cancel the rest of the races this year." Normally he would have referred to me as "Sarge," but he was so excited he hardly knew his own name.

"Simon certainly can't drive. There is not more that can be done," Rose responded.

"I asked him if I could drive. He told me about the promise he made to you and he said no, but I know I can do it. Is it okay if I drive, Mom?"

Rose looked at me, then back to Mike. "Mike, I don't think so."

"Please, Mom, I don't ask for much. Please say yes, please, please."

Rose returned to me. "Simon, what do you think?"

"As far as I am concerned, I am bound by my promise to you. It was never part of the deal for any of the boys to drive."

"But do you think he can do it? If you do, I won't hold you to that promise. It's up to you."

"Rose, you are placing a huge responsibility on me. Also, I don't know if he has what it takes to drive in competition."

"If you think he can, it's okay with me."

"We'll take the car to The Pines this weekend and see how he does. The track is not being used this week. Now is a perfect time for a trial run."

Mike yelled, "Semper Fi, Sarge!"

"Mike, that was not a yes, it was a maybe."

Saturday we put the Allard on the trailer and made the twenty-mile drive to The Pines. It was a beautiful day and quiet at the track. Rose drove the truck and Mike could not stop talking. I had never seen him like this before. We rolled the car off the trailer and Mike got in and started the engine. He had heard that sound many times before, but I could tell by the look on his face the sound was music in his ears. After the engine had warmed up, I signaled to turn it off. The car was loud and he couldn't have heard me.

Mike turned off the ignition and said, "I am ready to go!"

"Just slow down a bit. When racing you must think clearly and not get excited. Take a few slow laps, like you were driving your mom to church. Get the feel of the car, before you go all out. Don't let your head get ahead of the car. After that, pick up the pace, and after you have a feel of the track, give it all you've got. Push the car hard into the turns. When you think you want to brake, count to three and then brake hard to the middle of the turn and then back on the gas. Brake and accelerate, never coast."

I handed him a set of earplugs, goggles, and a helmet. He put them on like a gladiator preparing to enter the arena. If he was nervous, it didn't show. I know I was nervous and I'm sure Rose was. Rose picked up the stopwatch as Mike started the engine. He headed onto the track as Rose and I took a position at the start/finish line. Mike did exactly as I instructed him. After a few casual laps and few faster ones, I wrote on the small chalkboard we used to communicate with the driver, "Go!" I had seen messages on that pit board from Rose many times. I felt strange showing them to Mike. Rose started keeping his times on the lap chart. After about ten hot laps, she showed me his times.

"How did he do?"

He had started out a little slow as I had instructed and he continued to improve each lap. Rose could see the times and she knew they were good.

"His last laps were three seconds better than the course record! I think I've lost my job." I wrote on the board "bring it in."

Back in the pits, he brought the car to a stop in front of Rose and me. He removed the helmet and ear plugs and shouted, "How did I do?" After running a car with open exhaust, you get a little deaf temporarily. He didn't know he was shouting.

I tried to not show too much excitement. I gave him the thumbs-up and said, "You did good, Mike."

But Rose could not contain her excitement and her response was a total surprise to me. "Mike, your last laps were faster than the record."

Mike looked at me and by now I couldn't hide my feelings either. I smiled and said, "You did very good, son. Let's go home and get ready for Pebble Beach." I had never called him son before.

I made the announcement on Monday that we would be racing after all with Mike driving. "Semper Fi, Mike" was their reply. This was their sign of approval. We didn't have much work to do on the car, except placing an "X" with masking tape beside the numbers on the car. This identified the driver as a rookie and the other driver would be aware.

MIKE'S FIRST RACE

We had a full weekend of events. Mike's excitement was like a boy on Christmas morning seeing the new bike under the tree that he had asked Santa for or getting that Red Rider BB gun. Mike was older now and his dreams were different, but the excitement was the same. Pebble Beach Road Races are run on the roads winding through the Del Monte Forest. This was probably not the best track for Mike's debut, but this was the hand he was dealt. Mike was disappointed with his results in the preliminary event on Saturday. Personally, I thought he did very well against the veteran drivers and some new, more sophisticated cars. Mike thought, no he knew, he could do better and for the main event Sunday he was determined to prove it.

There were thirty cars in the race and as a rookie Mike was in the back of the field. In front were some C-Type Jags and Ferraris. Jaguar built just fifty-three of the fabulous

150 mph C-Type sports racing car, which won the 24-hour LeMans race in 1951. These were the latest cars from Europe and driven by some of the best drivers. Mike would have his hands full with the quality of cars and drivers in this field. Determined not to be humiliated again, he drove with a mission. I have never seen a young driver race with more ease. The car and he became one. He was driving like a veteran of many years' experience.

The event was a three-hour race and there was plenty of time to be patient. Mike drove every lap as if it were the last. After half an hour, Mike was running in the top ten. Still not satisfied, he increased his speed and moved steadily to fifth place. Rose was charting Mike's times and I was keeping the times on the Jag. Rose reported Mike's lap times to me and he was running consistent times of three seconds faster than the lead car. I was happy but concerned the car wouldn't hold up to that pace. I told Rose to give him the "EZ" sign. She did and his lap times dropped another second.

At the end of the second hour, he was ten seconds behind the lead C-Jag and was one second faster on lap times. If the car held up, he would be able to catch the Jag. I held my breath and hoped the car would last because Mike was not going to slow down and settle for second place. Near the end of the race, Mike was in the Jag's slipstream. This requires confidence in yourself and the driver in front of you. A slight mistake by either could be disaster for both. Mike had never done this before and I was worried. When they came around the next lap, Mike was so close to the Jag it looked like he was being towed. I don't know where or when Mike passed the Jag on the backside of the track, but he was ahead of the Jag and opening up the gap between them. When Mike took the checkered flag, I jumped to my feet and grabbed Rose. I kissed her long and hard on the lips. As soon as the pain hit my foot, I realized what I had done. I let her go and said, "Rose, I'm sorry. I shouldn't have done that."

She gave a stern look and replied, "No, you shouldn't have." Then she smiled. "You should have done it a long time ago."

All of the sudden, the pain left my foot and I felt really good. This was a day that dreams are made of. Mike realized his dream that day and I had mine. Both of us would remember this day, but for totally different reasons. I could understand Mike's joy; however, I don't know if he could understand mine.

ROMANCE AT LAST

Late Sunday evening after the celebrating was done,
well almost, we loaded the trucks and trailers for the trip
home. We had purchased two new 1952 Chevrolet
Suburbans and two covered trailers with the money John
had provided for us. One trailer was for the car and the
other trailer was outfitted with shop supplies and extra
parts.

Billy Williams, one of the boys or Bing as we called him,
drove the truck pulling the car. Mike was in the front seat
with Bing, and Rose and I were in the back seat. The
remaining boys were in the second truck with the supplies.
John was at all the races and was in his Cadillac driven by
his chauffeur. Bing was singing as usual and Mike was
reliving the three-hour race. I tried to listen to what he was
saying, but all I could think of was "the kiss." Rose and I
were holding hands and gazing into each other's eyes like
teenagers.

We arrived back at the shop around one in the morning. Mike had noticed that Rose and I had been very quiet during the trip home. He could tell something was different. I had scarcely heard a word he had said. It was very late and we didn't take time to unload anything, everyone just headed home.

Rose said goodnight and left Mike and I alone. Mike asked, "Sarge, is everything okay? You and Mom were very quiet during the trip back and you both seemed to be in a different world tonight."

"Mike, I'm sorry that I wasn't listening tonight, but things couldn't be better. Tomorrow we can talk, you can tell me about the race again and I will try to explain my behavior tonight."

"Do you want me to take you home now?"

"No, it's late. I'll just stay here at the shop tonight." The shop had a very comfortable sofa and a shower. I had spent the night there many times before so I kept clean clothes on hand. "Goodnight, Mike. I'll see you in the morning."

"Goodnight, Sarge."

I headed for the shop and Mike turned toward the house. I stopped and turned around. "Mike!" After a brief pause, "You did very well today and I'm proud of you!"

I tried to settle in for the night, but my mind was in overdrive. I had girlfriends in the past and some had been serious. I was thirty-five and had never come close to the altar in the past. I think that was all about to change. I had feelings for Rose from the beginning, but never acted on them. I think I had loved her from the first time we met. Now all I could think of was "the kiss."

I managed a couple of hours of sleep before the alarm went off at half past five the next morning. I wanted to go on my morning jog, but that's hard to do with your foot in a cast. Thank goodness I would be rid of it in another few weeks. Instead I prepared for the day ahead. I had just finished getting ready when Rose knocked and came in with a tray of hot coffee and breakfast. "Rose, good morning. You didn't have to bring me breakfast." I was glad she did and I was happy to see her first thing in the morning. "Did you sleep last night?" I asked.

She responded, "Not much. How 'bout you?"

"No, not much." I wanted to take her in my arms and kiss her again, oh...how I wanted to kiss her.

"Simon, what are you thinking about right now? At this very moment. What do you want to do?"

I walked over to her and put my arms around her and kissed her softly. "That's what I wanted to do and it's what I want to do for the rest of my life. Rose, I love you and I have for a long time. From the first day we met, I was captivated by your grace, charm, and unbelievable beauty. I've never said anything in fear that if we had a relationship it might somehow affect the relationship that I have established with Mike. But from that day, I knew my future was in your hands."

"I can understand your concerns, but I wish I had known how you felt and maybe we could have worked on our relationship together. I was hoping you felt that way because that is what I am feeling too. I love you."

"We need to talk about were we go next, I mean in our relationship. I want to date and court you and...how is

Mike going to feel about it?"

"I don't know how Mike will respond. However, we can no longer be 'just friends.' Come for dinner tonight and we'll tell Mike and John how we feel. Do you remember our first dinner together? We stared at each other, all the while hoping the other had not noticed. John noticed and the next morning he said, 'Rose, you are going to marry that man,' and I replied to him, 'John, I hope so—nothing would make me happier.'"

"Do I remember? Are you kidding? That was the night I fell in love. I knew that somehow we would get together. My concern for Mike only delayed what I hoped would happen from the beginning. I guess I better get to school. Rose, I love you and can't wait until tonight."

"Simon, you have made me so very happy and I'm glad to feel alive again. Now get out of here and rush back to me tonight. I love you!"

Monday was the longest day of my life. All I could think about was Rose and "the kiss." During lunch I went to the school office to call Rose. "Rose, this is Simon. I just had to hear your voice. Are you busy today?"

"No, I'm not busy. The cook and I are planning the menu for tonight. We're having your favorite, roasted lamb with mint jelly."

"That's great!" This would only be the second time in my life I'd had roasted lamb. "I can't wait for tonight and at the same time I'm a little nervous about what Mike and John might think."

"Don't worry about what they think, just remember that I love you and that's all that's important."

"Rose, I love you too. Listen, I'm going to let you get back to the menu. I can't wait for us to be together this evening. I love you. See you tonight."

I continued to go through the motions the rest of the day. After the afternoon class with the boys, Mike offered me a ride. "Sarge, Mom says you're coming for dinner tonight. What's the occasion?"

He caught me off guard; I felt he knew something was going on. "Oh, nothing really. Rose and I just have some things to discuss with you and John, that's all."

I went to the shop to shower, shave, and change clothes. A few minutes before seven, I made my way over to the house. Dinner was wonderful; the cook had made the lamb even better than before. Maybe love just made it taste better. After dinner we made ourselves comfortable in the parlor. John settled into his favorite chair and each of us took a seat. Mike sat in the chair next to his grandfather while Rose and I sat on the sofa.

John broke a brief silence. "I'm old enough and wise enough to know this was not just another dinner. Somebody tell me what's going on!" He looked first at Rose and me, then to Mike. "Don't all of you speak at once, somebody say something."

Rose started to speak. "John, I…that is we have…"

I interrupted and said, "Rose, let me tell them." I paused for a moment and continued. "After the race yesterday, something happened that both of you need to be aware of. In the excitement of Mike's victory…" There was another pause for me to think of exactly how I wanted to say this. All that came out was, "I kissed Rose and at that moment

I realized that I have loved her for a long time. We talked about it briefly this morning and she says she loves me as well. Rose and I have much to think about and talk over. We wanted both of you to know what happened Sunday and how we feel about each other."

Everyone just looked at each other for a moment before Mike broke the silence. "Sarge, how could you!" Then he smiled. "For a man so fast in a race car—how could you have taken so long to find out what a wonderful woman my mom is? All I can say is it's about time!"

John responded, "Simon, the first time I met you I could see that Rose saw something in you. I saw that same look in her eye the first time Richard brought her home to meet me. When Richard was killed, I thought that look was gone forever. I know you will be happy. I'm happy for both of you."

John and Mike excused themselves to leave Rose and me alone.

As Mike was leaving the room, I said, "Mike, you still haven't told me about the finish of the race."

Mike smiled and said, "Another time, Sarge, another time. It wasn't nearly as exciting as your news. Goodnight, Mom. Sarge, I'll see you in class tomorrow. Now don't you two stay up too late. Remember, tomorrow is a school day. Goodnight, Sarge."

We didn't take Mike's advice. After Mike and John went upstairs, I asked, "Rose do you believe in love at first sight?"

"No, I don't think that I do, do you?"

"A few years ago I would have said no. But now, yes I do. When I met you the first time and I learned a little about you, I could not get you off my mind. When you told me there were no men in your life, my thoughts took me to a world of fantasy. I wanted to know all about you, your goals, your happiness, as well as your sadness. I was saddened when you told me about Richard's death. I could see how deeply you loved him and I longed to see that look in your eyes for me. I wanted to take all of your sadness and turn it to joy. During the past two years, many times I wanted to respond to my feelings. You are so beautiful, but that is not what attracted me to you. You are so much more than just a good-looking woman. The way you conduct yourself in a crowd or with individuals has always impressed me. You don't dwell on problems. You solve them. You are a most impressive woman. I believe I loved you from that very first meeting."

"I have similar feelings for you, but not from the beginning. There were times, more in the last six months, that I hoped something would happen between us. I'm not sure exactly when I realized that I had fallen in love with you. It was more of a gradual process with me. I do know how much you mean to me now and I want you to be in my life forever. I could tell from the beginning that you were a man of great character. I was very impressed that you cared enough about Mike to help him."

Rose and I continued to talk for hours. It was almost two in the morning before we said goodnight and I went to the shop for a few hours sleep. I was happy that we had our feelings out in the open now.

CHRISTMAS

This year will be our first Christmas together as a couple. Since my dad passed away, the season hasn't been much of a celebration for me. I quickly learned that Christmas was a big deal to Rose. The house had to be decorated inside and out with great care. Lucky for me, that was left to professionals. In the front yard was a nativity scene that included a few live animals. If Rose could have found people willing, she would have had them in the scene also. I was at a loss for a gift for her. She was a lady of means and had all that she desired; I was a teacher of little means. What could I offer her that she didn't have? We had only been dating three months, but I knew that I wanted to spend the rest of my life with her. I was ready to ask her to marry me. I think we both knew that would come; however, the question had not been asked. I decided to propose to her on Christmas Eve. My dad had kept my mother's rings and the engagement ring had a nice-sized stone. My mom and dad had been married for seven years before he had enough money to purchase the rings. I hoped Rose would not mind an antique ring.

The Brock family has a large party each Christmas Eve and this would be my first year to attend. I had taken the rings to a jeweler to have them cleaned and the settings tightened. The guests had gathered in the family room and the party was into the second hour. I asked Rose if I could see her in the parlor for a moment.

"Rose, I want to give you your Christmas gift tonight in private."

"Simon, your gift is under the tree, don't you want to wait?"

I took her hand and led her to the parlor. "No, what I have for you can't wait. I have something to ask you. I am afraid I'm no good at this." We were both sitting on the sofa; I got up and knelt down in from of her and picked up her left hand. "I don't have any experience at this, so I'll just ask." I looked into her beautiful blue eyes. "Rose, will you marry me?"

Rose yelled, "Yes!" loud enough for the guests in the other room to hear. I placed the ring on her finger and she looked at it for a long time. I believed she was thinking how small it was, but that was not at all what she was thinking.

"Simon, my mother had a ring very similar to this and I always thought it was so very special and now I have one of my own. It is exactly what I wanted for Christmas. It makes the house shoes I got you seem kinda cheap!"

I had no idea what she had for me, but I was pretty sure it wasn't house shoes.

Of course when we returned to the party, all eyes were on us. Rose blurted out, "Simon and I are getting married."

One by one for the rest of the evening we were being congratulated. After the guests had gone for the night, we exchanged the rest of the gifts. Rose gave John a set of first edition mystery books that he wanted. John gave her a new mink coat. She may not be able to use it much in southern California, but it would be nice for trips to Europe later. Mike gave his mom a diamond bracelet and she gave him a new Hi-Fi system and a ring. It was not just any ring; it was his father's Marine Corps ring. She also gave him his father's wings. She had saved my gift for last. The box was large and heavy. I opened the box to find a few bricks and another box. I proceeded to open it, another box to open after that. I don't recall how many boxes there were, but I ended up with a box about three inches square. Inside was a gold keychain with a key on it.

"You'll have to go to the shop to see what it fits!"

The four of us made our way to the shop. It was a nice warm night and we walked slow enough for John to keep up. I opened the door and a beautiful car filled my eyes. There was a new red two-door hardtop 1952 Cadillac with red interior. I've never had a new car before and never did I dream of one this nice. My old Chevrolet truck was going into retirement for sure.

Rose asked, "Do you want to go for a drive, big boy?"

"Yeah, let's go for a spin!" I opened the door for Rose and she got in, sliding to the middle of the seat. I sat down in the beautiful red leather seat that seemed to have been made just for me. We drove to the beach with Rose sitting close to me with her head on my shoulder. The car was great and I loved Rose and she loved me. What more could a man want from life? This was the best Christmas of my life!

We returned to the house around eleven that night. John and Mike had already retired for the night. Rose and I spent two more hours sharing our dreams for the future and contemplating that future together. We were happy but realistic at the same time. Marriage is a blend of personalities and backgrounds, making compromise a necessity for both of us. We agreed that the Brock Estate was the logical place for us to make our home. Rose wanted our wedding to be held in the garden and I thought that would be very nice. The guest list, flowers, food, and entertainment for the wedding were all discussed. There was much to be done and decisions to be made and one night could not address them all. It would be great if life were a fairy tale and we would live happily ever after. Tonight we are extremely happy and I didn't want the night to end.

1952 LeMans

It felt good to be officially engaged. John insisted on giving us a big party to announce our engagement. He rented a banquet room at the Hotel Del Coronado for the party in early February 1952. It became one of San Diego's largest social events of the year. He tracked down some of my old buddies from the war to surprise me. But the biggest surprise would come at the close of the evening. As the evening was drawing to a close, John called one of his "emergency meetings." He moved to the bandstand and took the microphone. "Friends, we are here tonight to celebrate the engagement of Rose to Simon Spangler. Most of you don't know about the special place we have for Simon in our family. Simon is a high school teacher at Mission Bay, a very good high school teacher. The kind of teacher that makes a difference in young people's lives. When Mike first went to his class, Mike was on the road to destruction. There was nothing Rose or I could do. Simon saw something in Mike and five other boys in his class and began to mentor them. In two short years he has turned six deadbeat boys headed in the wrong direction into the finest in their class."

From my cheering section off to the right I heard, "Semper Fi!" My "would be" Marines always had something to say.

John laughed and continued. "As an engagement gift to Rose and Simon, I am taking them to France for a little race at LeMans. Now I am an old man and I don't get around very well these days, so I'm taking Mike and the boys with us to help chaperon these two lovebirds. Mike and the other boys are about to finish their junior year. It will be the boys' reward for their hard work in the last two years."

Nowadays I am very rarely at a loss for words and I added, "John, I'm pretty crafty, do you think the seven of you are enough troops?"

"Simon, if we're not, Rose can do the rest." That brought a good laugh from the guests.

One of my dreams was to attend the 24-Hour LeMans race. I was looking forward to the trip and I'm sure the boys were also. The best part would be spending time with Rose. Mike had been to Europe several times with Rose and his grandfather, but the experience would be the first for me and the boys. I could sense their anticipation in class and around the shop in the evenings.

We arrived in Paris on Saturday June the seventh, a week before the race. Our hotel, Artus Hotel, was located at 34, rue de Buci. Rose and I started our Saturday evening sipping coffee at the Café Le Paris, a sidewalk café on ave des Champs Elysees and watching the tourists and locals go about their business. The geraniums hanging from balcony rails added a perfect touch. Paris is crowded with narrow roads. No one gets in a hurry, life is relaxed as families and couples enjoyed the long sunlit evening.

Rose and I planned our tours while John was content to read the books Rose had given him for Christmas. The boys made their plans to see Paris as only young men can do. They are all good young men and they managed to stay out of trouble. Rose and I started Sunday with a trip to the Eiffel Tower and the Arc-de-Triomphe. We took a boat along the Seine. On Monday we took a tour of Notre Dame. Paris has an abundance of museums and we saw as many as possible on Tuesday. The best part was being with Rose; often we would stop at a sidewalk café and talk. This is the way I wanted life to be. As long as time was spent in the company of my sweet Rose, I'd be happy. Paris is called the City of Light and is said to be created for lovers. It certainly was for Rose and me.

Wednesday afternoon we took a train to LeMans, 150 miles southwest of Paris. The countryside was beautiful as the train made its way through vineyard after vineyard. During the trip, the boys filled us in on their stay in Paris. They were having a marvelous time. There were smiles on everyone's faces because we all were having a wonderful time. John saw how good things were going and he was the happiest of all knowing he had done a good thing for his family.

We arrived at the Hotel Chantecler at 50 Rue Pelouse in LeMans on Wednesday afternoon. We settled into our rooms and started getting dressed for dinner. Every day was filled with surprises and pleasant experiences. That evening we were dining at La Grand-rue restaurant when John spotted a man in a white dinner jacket walk in. John raised his hand and shouted, "Briggs, over here!" This was a quiet, upscale French restaurant and the gentleman had no trouble hearing John. He walked over to our table. The boys and I stood as the gentleman approached our table. Because of his condition, John remained seated.

"Briggs, I want you to meet my family, well, my extended family. This is Rose and her fiancé, Simon Spangler. My grandson, Michael Brock, and the other lads are Bob Varner, Billy Williams, Chester Walker, Perry and Jerry Griffon. This is Briggs Cunningham, a friend of mine from the east coast."

Mr. Cunningham replied, "It's a pleasure to meet each of you. Simon, you are one lucky man. Rose is very stunning."

Rose blushed a little and said, "Mr. Cunningham, thanks for the compliment and I think I'm the lucky one."

John asked, "Briggs, are you meeting anyone for dinner tonight?"

"No, I gave my crew a little time away from the boss and I will be dining alone."

"Please, join us."

"Thanks, that's very kind of you, I would be happy to."

I was thrilled to be sharing a table with Briggs Cunningham. Mr. Cunningham is a well-known car owner and driver from the east coast. He was bringing a new car of his own design to LeMans this year after having some success here the last two years. In 1950 he brought two Cadillacs; Briggs and Phil Walters drove a stock Cadillac similar to the one Rose gave me for Christmas. His car was nicknamed "Clumsy Puppy." The only modification it had was a dual carb manifold. Sam and Miles Collier drove the other, a specially designed aerodynamic body that acquired the name "Le Monstre." It captured the imagination of the French fans because its huge engine caused the ground to shake and the exhaust would spew flames out of the exhaust at night. The entries were memorable but clearly not capable of winning. The coupe finished tenth and Le Monstre finished eleventh after losing time hitting a sandbank. In 1951 he returned with the first of his Cunningham roadsters, the C-2R. They all failed to finish for various reasons. They were much more successful back home on the road courses in the States. This year he had his new C-4R with Hemi engine, the same engine we were using in our Allard.

"Mr. Cunningham, I noticed the program for the race features a painting of your C-4 trailing a C-type Jag," I noted.

"Mr. Spangler, please call me Briggs. In view of our results the last two years, I should take it as a compliment. However, I hope to see my cars finish one and two. I understand that you and these young men have done some road racing."

"Yes, we go racing a little, about three or four events a year. We have an Allard with Hemi power."

"Mr. Spangler," Briggs started and I interrupted, "Please, call me Simon."

He continued. "Simon, you don't need to tell me of your lad's exploits. Mike's win at Pebble Beach quickly reached the east coast. Those veteran drivers didn't like a rookie beating them to the checkered flag, especially in a car that shouldn't be able to keep up with theirs."

Mike responded, "Thanks, Mr. Cunningham. Your kind words are appreciated. Being a rookie, I didn't know what was expected of me."

Mike was joking and Mr. Cunningham laughed along with the others. All the boys will remember their experience that night. I know I will.

As Briggs stood to leave after dinner he spoke to Mike. "Mike, how would you like to take a few laps around the track with me tomorrow?"

"Are you kidding? Yes, that would be great, when?"

"I'll give all of you pit passes for the week. Come by about eight o'clock in the morning."

Thursday and Friday were practice days. Mike, the boys, Rose, and I arrived at the track a few minutes before eight. We all wished we were the ones getting to take laps with Mr. Cunningham, but Mike was the lucky one; we went as spectators only. Briggs and his crew had the car warmed up for practice. Mike put on a crash helmet and climbed into the passenger seat. As soon as they were buckled in, the pit crew gave a thumbs-up and the fun started for Mike. Briggs took Mike on five laps before returning to the pits. I've seen Mike excited many times before, but I've never seen him this excited. I'm sure he had visions of driving the race himself.

Mike gave us all the details on his return. "By the first turn, Dunlop Curve, we were in top gear. Mr. Cunningham downshifted to second gear and took the turn about 60 mph. The elevation decreases as we exited 'Dunlop' and we accelerated reaching fourth gear before we got to Esses, immediate left and right corners in third gear at about 100 mph. After the Esses we encountered the Tertre Rouge, a right-hand corner. Mr. Cunningham said it was one of the most important corners on the course. It's the last corner before the first long straightaway. We came out of the turn very fast. We reached top gear and we were doing 140 mph before the Chicane (L'Arche). Mr. Cunningham hit the brakes hard going in, downshifted to second gear; we were doing about 60 mph in the turn. On the second straight we reached about 120 mph before we hit the next chicane, La Florandiere, at about 60 mph. We accelerated out to complete the last third of the backstretch of the racetrack. Very hard braking to Mulsanne Corner, down to first gear, slowing to 45 mph. The Mulsanne straight followed, which is four miles long, we reached top speed around 160 mph. For the Indianapolis turn, we slowed to 80 mph to make it. Then very quickly we slowed to third gear to make the left-hand corner. We carried decent speed through here because there is banking to the corner, that's why it's named Indianapolis. We took the Arnage turn about 40 mph. We accelerated to a long straight flat out through the next series of turns. Mr. Cunningham said this is a tricky part of the track and you can make up a lot of time here. Only concrete walls and guardrail greet you if you make a mistake. This area is run about 100 mph. After a short straight there are several turns before downshifting to first gear. We accelerated and crossed the start/finish line. All this took less than five minutes covering the 8.38 miles. I can't imagine doing this for 24 hours. I love it."

"Mike, would you like to drive the track yourself?" Briggs asked.

Mike looked at me in disbelief and responded to Briggs, "I would like that very much, but I might damage your car."

"Don't worry about that, I'll be in the passenger seat keeping an eye on you. I want to see how you handle yourself in a race car. Grab the wheel and let's see what you've got."

Mike was uncertain whether to accept the invitation, but he finally said, "Okay, let's do it!" and climbed into the car.

The two of them took five more laps and returned to the pits. Mike was even happier than before.

After returning to the pits Briggs told Mike, "I was very impressed with what I saw in you. You have a future in road racing."

"Thanks, Mr. Cunningham, coming from you that is a very high compliment."

For the Cunningham team, it was time to get to serious work preparing for the race. As we were leaving I overheard one of the pit crew tell Briggs, "I don't know if

I should tell you this, but his last two laps were five seconds faster than your best time in practice."

"I knew he was quick, but not quite that fast. He's going to drive for me someday!"

LeMans is a great event with a carnival atmosphere. Over 200,000 spectators will attend the event this year. Friday was Parade day. We arrived at the track early Saturday. The pre-race activity never slowed down including the "ear of corn," which is the traditional LeMans start. The ear of corn was the signal for the drivers to run to their car, jump in, and go racing. At four o'clock Saturday afternoon, the drivers sprinted to their cars and the race was under way. The boys and I didn't leave until eight p.m. Sunday night, four hours after the race ended.

The C-4K coupe of Cunningham's team driven by John Fitch and George Rice took the lead in the early laps, but retired in the eighth hour due to engine failure. Of the fifty-eight cars that started the race, only seventeen finished. Mercedes-Benz took the top two spots with their 300 SL, followed by a Nash-Healey. The winning 300 SL covered 277 laps, over 2320 miles, during the 24 hours; that's over 96 mph average each lap. The Cunningham C-4R driven by Briggs and Bill Spears finished fourth with Briggs driving 20 of the 24 hours.

LeMans was a terrific experience, but with every great trip the time comes when you must go home. I think John got tired of me saying "thank you." Attending a LeMans road race had been a dream of mine for many years and he had made that dream come true. Spending time with Rose and the race was—well it's just beyond words.

On the plane returning to California, Mike asked me, "Do you think you and I will race at LeMans someday?"

"It takes a lot of money to race here—but who knows what the future might bring. We just might make it back as competitors. Who knows?"

SENIOR YEAR

We had four races scheduled for this year. My broken foot healed, but a little stiffness remained. I could have resumed the driving duties; however, Mike is a much better driver than I had ever been. I drove a car, but Mike is an extension of the automobile. He is that perfect blend of man and machine. Racing comes as natural as breathing for him. The season will begin and end at Torrey Pines with March AFB and Pebble Beach sandwiched in between. Mike started where he left off last season with an easy win at Torrey Pines. He had lapped every car in the field except the one in second and was only about 100 feet behind it as the checkered flag fell. We had engine problems at March AFB and settled for a fourth place finish. We had burned a piston and finished the race on seven cylinders. The engine would have to be rebuilt before Pebble Beach.

Before the next race at Pebble Beach, Mike received a call from Mr. Cunningham asking if he would drive for him at LeMans in June. Of course his answer was "yes" without asking his mother for permission

Pebble Beach was a much-anticipated event for Mike. Returning to the track of his rookie race and first victory was like it had happened only yesterday. Mike won the preliminary race on Saturday and was on the front row for the start of Sunday's race. After the six-hour event, we had a second place finish.

A second race at Torrey Pines had been added this year. The event was only three weeks before our wedding and Rose had everything planned. The race would be a good time for her to relax and have some fun. Mike was determined to win the race this weekend. Three hours into the race, Mike was in second place chasing a C-type Jaguar. On the back part of the track, the lead Jag's drive shaft broke. As the shaft dug into the pavement it ruptured the fuel tank. The driver hit the brakes hard sending fuel into the cockpit. When the fuel reached the exhaust pipe, the car burst into flames. Mike tried to avoid the accident but lost control of the Allard and ultimately crashed.

We could see smoke from the fire as the speaker announced an accident involving the number 5 Jag and the number 13 Allard. Rose and I jumped in the truck and rushed to the site. We arrived on the scene as the track officials and medics were loading both drivers in the ambulance. By the time they reached the hospital, the driver of the Jag had died. Mike was alive, but barely. All

Rose could do was cry, sobbing uncontrollably. I tried to comfort her but she pulled away.

Mike had been in surgery for two hours before the doctor came out to give us the news. "Mrs. Brock, your son has very serious injuries. He has two broken legs and multiple internal injuries. We have repaired the internal injuries and set the legs. However, he has a head injury as well and has swelling of the brain. We will try all we can do to reduce the swelling; then the only thing left to do is wait."

Rose spoke for the first time since the accident. "Wait for what?"

"Wait for him to regain consciousness."

Mike remained in a coma for a week and Rose never left his side. I would leave only to talk to John and the boys. I would bring Rose something to eat, but she ate very little.

After the first week Rose spoke her first words to me. She turned and looked at me as she removed her ring from her finger. "Simon, I can't marry you. If you had never started this racing thing, Mike would not be here today. I don't want to see you anymore." She handed me her ring.

"Rose, I'm so sorry." It was easy to see that she blamed me for the accident and maybe I did myself. I could have argued my case, but that would cause her more pain.

"Rose, I'm sorry that you feel that way. I suppose that it would be best that I just leave now." I was hoping that she would say no, I have changed my mind, please stay. But she didn't say a word.

"Rose, I am truly sorry that we have to end this way.

Goodbye, Rose. If you don't mind I would like to call John and get reports about Mike's condition."

"Yes, Simon, that's fine. Please go now!"

I walked slowly from the room, still hoping she would ask me to stay. Before leaving the hospital, I stopped by the chapel and offered a prayer for Mike and Rose.

Shortly John came in and spoke, "Simon, am I interrupting?"

"No, John, please come in. I could use the company."

"Rose told me what she had told you and I wanted to catch you before you left the hospital. Simon, you know that I am a deeply religious man. I have faith that your prayers will be answered. Rose is hurting now and she didn't mean what she said. Give her the space she needs and in time, things will be fine. Try not to worry and don't blame yourself." John's advice was to be patient.

"Try not to worry! That's going to be difficult. I do blame myself for the accident because I didn't resume the responsibilities for driving when my foot healed. It was just that Mike was so much better at it than me. I don't know what to do—I am lost without Rose. John, call me if there are any changes in Mike's condition and keep me up to date. Someone once said, 'It is better to have loved and lost, than to have never loved at all.' Whoever said that hadn't loved nor lost in my opinion. Well, anyway, thanks for visiting with me, I guess I'll go home and—well, I don't know what I'll do when I get there. Thanks again, call me please."

I left the hospital with my thoughts about my comments about love and losing love. Without allowing love, people could shield themselves from the pain of love lost. Then again they would never experience the joys that love brings. Maybe there is some truth to the saying. I had to remind myself that the pain I was having could not be compared to the pain Rose was feeling as Mike lay in a coma. I had never been more in love than I was with Rose; losing her was like a part of me had been removed. If Rose lost Mike, her pain would be much greater than my pain. Knowing her pain only made mine worse. Mike simply must survive for all of us.

DREAMS SHATTERED

I went through the motions each day trying to make sense of what was happening and where I would go from here. I had a responsibility to my students and maybe work would help me get my mind off my problems. It was a noble thought, but it didn't help. I hadn't given up on Rose and me, but things were not looking good for us. The brief time we had together was, without a doubt, the best of my life and I didn't want to go back to the life I had before Rose. I was concerned for Mike and I was blaming myself for the incident. If I could turn back the clock, what would I change? If I had not become involved with Mike, I would have never met Rose and found the love of my life. If this, if I…everything was a big if. Life without Rose was almost more than I could bear. I called John every day to get a report on Mike and Rose. Each day his reply was, "There is no change in Mike's condition. Rose remains by his side and needs rest. I wish she would talk to you, I know that would be a big help to her. I'm afraid she is being very stubborn. Give her more time!"

The boys came by and tried to cheer me up. They knew what Rose had said about the accident. They were sorry about Mike's accident, but not about the racing.

One of the boys told me, "You took six failing boys and turned them into straight 'A' students and for that we will always be thankful. You were not responsible for the accident and Mrs. Brock will see that eventually. Mike is going to recover and we'll all get back to normal." I was so far out of it; I'm not sure which one was talking.

"Thanks, guys, I hope you are right." I managed to acknowledge their valiant attempt to cheer me up.

Billy said, "We took the car back to the shop and it is a twisted mess. A track official filled us in on the details of the accident. Do you want me to tell you about it?"

I responded, "Yes, maybe knowing what happened would help. I would like to know what happened."

"This is what the track official told us: 'When the Jag lost its drive shaft, the fuel tank ruptured and it burst into flames, filling the entire track with fire. Mike drove through the fire to find a car stalled in front of him. He tried to avoid contact with that car, but clipped the back of it and spun out of control. The Allard rolled several times and then end over end before coming to rest upside down.'"

Rose and I saw the medics pull Mike and the other driver from the wreckage. The boys asked, "Sarge, when are you coming back to school? We have finals next week and we need you to help us prepare."

"I'll be back Monday." I felt Rose would forgive me eventually and we would get back together, but only if Mike survived. They hadn't told me anything different from what I thought. However, their words "we need you" helped get me back to a reality, although I knew they were well prepared for finals. Still I ached for Rose and for Mike to recover. I wanted so much to give Rose comfort and all my presence did was make her feel worse.

A week passed then another and Mike's condition remained unchanged. Our lives went on, although these were very sad times. The boys graduated and when Mike's name was called, they all walked across the stage to receive his diploma.

Mike was going into the fifth week of the coma. When I talked to John that week I asked, "John, will Rose talk to me yet?"

"Simon, she shows no signs of wanting to talk to anyone, especially you. Give her more time. She says very little to me. She won't eat much and I fear that she will get sick because of her run-down condition. She needs a break and she needs to get some rest." John didn't blame me for the accident, but he could do nothing to convince Rose.

On Wednesday of that week, Rose was holding Mike's hand as she felt a tug; he opened his eyes. "Mom, what's happened?" For the first time in over a month, the tears that Rose shed were tears of joy and not sadness.

"Mike, oh Mike. It's so good to hear your voice. We have so much to talk about, but right now I want the doctors to check you out!" Rose called for the doctors.

The doctors examined Mike and everything looked great. They told Rose he should make a full recovery. They left Rose and Mike to catch up on the last month.

"Mom, how long have I been out?"

"Over a month!" Rose replied.

"I missed my graduation. I was supposed to give a speech!"

"The principal read your speech to the class. I hope I had the final copy to give him. The entire class was moved by your speech or at least that's what I heard. I missed the graduation myself. The boys picked up your diploma, you did graduate."

"I missed your wedding too. Speaking of that, where's Sarge?"

"Oh, I cancelled the wedding and told Simon that I didn't want to see him anymore."

"What? Why? I believe that's the dumbest thing you have ever done. I know that you love him. What were you thinking?"

"Mike, it's hard to admit, but I felt he was responsible since he was the one that started you racing."

"Mom, that's just plain wrong. He wasn't going to let me race because of his promise to you. You released him from that promise at my urging. I heard you tell him that. To blame him is not right. Do you still love him?"

"Yes, I do, and I have missed him, but I didn't know how to make things right."

"Yes, you do. Just call him and tell him how you really feel."

"You're right, I shouldn't have blamed him, but he won't forgive me. I've hurt him too much."

"You don't know that until you talk with him. Just call him, Mom!"

"You're not going to rest 'til I call him, are you!"

"Nope, that's a fact. Call him."

"Okay, I'll call him."

"I don't mean when you get home and you are going home to get some rest. You look like you've been in the coma and I don't mean tomorrow or the next day. I mean call him now." Mike went on. "Do it now, there's the phone. I want you to get him here and you can talk this thing out with him."

It was late Wednesday night when my phone rang. "Simon, this is Rose." When she said Simon, I knew it was Rose. The voice of Rose coming over the phone was the sweetest sound I could imagine. I was filled with excitement to hear her voice and fearful that her news might be bad. The tone of her voice made me think the news was good.

"Rose, it's so good to hear your voice. Please give me good news."

"Yes, the news is good. Mike is awake and is going to be fine. But he has been on my case pretty good for breaking our engagement. Could you come to the hospital so we can talk? I know it's late and Mike is not going to give me any peace until he sees you and we try to patch things up."

"There is nothing to patch up! I'll be there in fifteen minutes! Rose, I love you!"

"Simon, I love you too, please hurry."

My feet would not move fast enough for me to get to the hospital. This day turned out to be a good day, a very good day.

REBUILDING

I arrived at the hospital and rushed to Mike's room. I wanted to grab Rose and kiss her. But I spoke to Mike first. "Mike, I'm glad you are going to be okay. I've been worried about you and your mom, she has not left your side for the past month."

"Thanks, Sarge. But you and Mom have a problem that needs to be addressed before you say anymore. Mom has been unfair to you. She has blamed you for the accident and—well, I'll be quiet and let Mom talk."

"Simon, Mike has pointed out, and rightly so, that his driving was as much my fault as yours. No, that's not right, you wouldn't have let him drive at all because of your promise to me. I have to accept full responsibility. I'm sorry for blaming you. I know that I hurt you and I'm sorry. Can you ever forgive me?"

"Rose, that doesn't matter now. There is nothing to forgive. The important thing is that Mike is going to be fine and I still love you."

"Simon, I do love you too. But I have one question for you. Will you marry me?"

"Rose, I just happen to have something in my pocket that belongs to you. It has been in my pocket ever since you removed it from your finger and gave it back to me. I wanted to keep it handy because I never gave up hope for this day." I pulled the ring from my pocket and placed it on her hand. "Yes, I would be thrilled to marry you. The sooner the better." I held her in my arms and never wanted to let her go. We kissed and that was about all the smooching Mike could stand.

Mike chimed in. "Okay, that's enough, you two. Catch your breath and spend some time with the patient now. I know you have lots of catching up to do but you'll have the rest of your life for that. Not to change the subject, but I'm not going to be able to compete at LeMans this year, am I?"

"Actually the race has been run. Mr. Cunningham said you could drive for him anytime you want. He was very sad to hear of your accident and has called me almost every day to check on your condition." As I told him, I could see disappointment on his face.

Mike was released from the hospital a week later to recuperate at home. Mike would be in a wheelchair for several weeks, but he would make a full recovery. Rose was glad to have him home and now she could get the rest that she badly needed. By the weekend, Mike was ready to look at the Allard. I rolled him to the shop and opened the door.

Mike wheeled himself inside and looked at the car. "It's going to be harder to rebuild this pile of scrap metal than rebuild your relationship with Mom."

"You and the boys are going away to school. Our racing days are finished. We can salvage the engine and scrap the rest."

"No! I don't want to do that. I want to rebuild it."

"Mike, it's not worth it and you will be busy with school and the others will also."

Mike responded, "I'm sure they will want to rebuild it too. It's just so much a part of our lives now and a symbol of how far we've come. We'll work on it during summer breaks until it's done."

"Okay, Mike, we'll start when you get better."

We worked on the car that summer, picking up where we left off the next summer. By the time the boys had graduated from college the car was restored. Our racing days were behind us so we restored it for street use. We dressed it up a bit with chrome wire wheels instead of the racing steel wheels. Mike likes to take it out when he wants to think.

Rose and I got married in January of 1954. Mike was my best man and the other boys were groomsmen. Rose and I honeymooned in Hawaii. It had been thirteen years since the attack on Pearl Harbor. I wanted to see Hawaii again and see it under better circumstances. Rose was with me this time and there was no war. How could circumstances be any better?

Mike went east to attend Harvard. Perry and Jerry Griffon went to the Naval Academy. Billy Williams and

Bob Varner joined the Marines after they graduated from USC. Chester Walker started acting after his graduation from Berkeley.

Twelve months after our wedding our daughter was born. Marilyn is the apple of her mother's eye and every bit as good looking as her mother. That's not just a father talking, that's a fact.

Mike graduated from Harvard in 1957 and we gave him a new Corvette with all the racing options for graduation. He talked me into preparing it for competition. After a few weeks, it was ready to race. Mike had not driven in competition since the accident, but was eager to race again. We took the car to Torrey Pines for some shakedown laps. Mike took about twenty laps before returning to the pit area. He turned off the ignition and said, "That's enough for me."

His lap times were very impressive and I thought he was ready to go racing. "Mike, there's a new track at Riverside. It's three weeks away, but I think we can be ready."

"Sarge, you didn't understand what I meant. I don't want to drive in competition again."

"Why? Your times were very good."

"I know, but everything that used to be second nature to me I have to think about now. I kept asking myself, do I downshift now? Is it time to brake? Maybe with time it would all come back. It all seemed unnatural to me."

"You could still be very competitive, but I think I understand. Let's go home."

We took the car back to the shop. Mike drove it on the street sometimes, but he never went racing again. The car is over twenty years old and has less than 10,000 miles on the odometer.

REVISITED

Rose and I have been married for twenty-six years now. Mike received an engineering degree and has a master's degree in business. He is forty-seven and running his grandfather's business. Mike married Billy's younger sister, Betty. Betty came to the shop often with her brother. She was and is a beautiful and charming young woman. They have given us three grandsons. Our daughter, Marilyn, is twenty-five and engaged to be married to one of the boys that I mentored years later. In her teens Marilyn was very competitive in tennis. She got that from her mom, not me. She and Rose share the love of tennis, just as Mike and I had with racing.

As I sit here in the shop Mike's grandfather built for us years ago, I often reflect on our life together. A corner of the shop has become our trophy room and my office retreat. The old Ford holds a place of honor in the middle, the Allard in which Mike won his first race on the right, fully restored, and our last race car, although it was never raced, the '57 Vette is on the left closest to my desk. The three grandsons are sitting in the cars and dreaming of racing around a track, just as their dad, my dad, and I did years ago. On the wall are photographs of my first class, "The Boys." I often come here and lean back in my chair with my feet on the desk looking at the cars and the photos. All the boys had nicknames and those names often appeared to be prophetic.

Bob Varner we called "Monkey." Bob was small in stature and often moved around like a small spider monkey. He started as "Grease Monkey" and was later shortened to "Monkey." Bob could always find and get grease on him. Bob served four years in the Marine Corps and is a veteran of Nam. Bob now owns a large chain of auto repair shops across the country.

Perry Griffon we called "Doc" when someone would smash a finger, get a cut or bruise, Doc would patch them up. His first diagnosis was my broken foot. Jerry, his twin brother, was "Preacher." He kept us on the straight and narrow. Both attended the Naval Academy, received their commission in the Marine Corps, and served in Vietnam. Doc is now a heart surgeon and Preacher is the pastor of one of the largest churches in the country.

Billy Williams was always happy and sang all the time. We called him "Bing." He was the heartthrob of all the girls in school. He was very good looking and had a voice like Bing Crosby. He could have had a singing career with the right agent. Billy also served as a Marine but didn't return from Vietnam and is still listed as missing in action. No matter where Billy is today, I'm sure he is still singing.

Chester Walker was the one that kept us laughing; he loved to play jokes and cut up. He was tall and lanky and the only one not to become a Marine. We called him "Joker," but he was the best mechanic of the bunch. He made a few movies and TV shows and later went into drag racing. He ran Top Fuel cars and was the NHRA National Champion four times and is now a consultant for Brock Automotive, the company Mike's grandfather started to fund our racing program. He also served in Nam in the Marine Corps.

All of "The Boys," as Rose called them, graduated from high school and college. Mike was valedictorian of his class, but never got to give his speech because of the accident. His picture is above the others next to mine.

John Michael "Mike" Brock II always seemed to be in charge and the boys called him "Boss." Mike has always been more than a stepson. Over the years he started calling me Dad and in one of our serious moments he told me, "You are honest and have a high code of integrity. That is the most important thing you taught me." I said almost exactly the same words about my father years ago. Mike became president of Brock Industries fifteen years ago when John passed away. Mike convinced me to become the CEO of Brock Automotive (BAI). BAI manufactures aftermarket-racing products and auto accessories. After Mike's crash, John started research to develop fire-resistant material for racing suits. That's now one of the items that we manufacture and sell. Now I call

Mike "Boss," but he will always be my favorite student and the son I never had. Shortly after he became president of Brock Industries, *Time* magazine was interviewing him and during the course of the interview, he was asked about his stepfather.

This was his reply: "As you have mentioned earlier, I am the son of a war hero and the grandson of one of the country's leading industrialists, but please don't refer to Simon Spangler as my stepfather. I mean no disrespect to my father or my grandfather, but Simon Spangler put me on the right track in life and the man I am today is the result of his mentoring, care, and love for me. To me he is and always will be my dad."

I always thought teaching was a profession with no rewards. I was wrong! Rose, my lovely bride of twenty-six years, remains the love of my life. She is just as beautiful today as she was the day we met. The life Rose and I have together and helping young men change their lives have been the greatest rewards any man could have. Although I left the teaching profession for the corporate world many years ago, I still mentor a group of young men from the high school at the shop on weekends. They bring their cars in for modifications or repairs. We don't go racing but they do love to hear the stories. As with most stories, they seem to get better with each telling. I often reflect on the days gone by and raise my soda glass to the photos on the wall and say, "Semper Fi, boys. Semper Fi."

Printed in the United States
47138LVS00002B/1

9 781413 745122